I0520135

Hidden
Deception

MYRA Y. PATTERSON

ISBN: 0615798780
ISBN-13: 978-0615798783

DEDICATION

This book is dedicated to "The Crew," and my little Jaden. Love you guys throughout all of eternity! Know that the sky is the limit and you can do all things through Christ who strengthens you! And to my dear friend June Black...FRIENDS FOR LIFE...love you much!

ACKNOWLEDGMENTS

First and foremost I give thanks to God for giving me the talent and ability to write. Although it doesn't seem like it by the verbiage written in the pages of this book, Jesus truly is my Lord and Savior. I Bless Him!

To my husband...I love you babe! Thank you so much for all your support. And to my four children whom I refer to as "The Crew", I love y'all more than anything. I pray that each of you will see and know that by watching me accomplish my goals, that you can do all things through Christ who strengthens you. And to my little Jaden, my grandson...I never knew love like this! You are YaYa's little man and my heartbeat! I love you more than you'll ever know. To my sweetie pies Lil Troy and Caleb, (grandbabies) YaYa loves you sooo much!

To my beloved and first cousin Vonne, you encouraged me so much and kept pouring into me year after year after year until the seed took root. And I can now say, "I did it." Thank you for never giving up on me even when I got on your nerves, especially when my OCD kicked in. You repeated things over and over and over again, having the patience of Job. LOL!!

And to my iQor babies...Lord knows I love y'all. When I say y'all are my babies I mean just that!

Lord knows y'all pulled on my heart strings! Y'all just stayed in trouble and only Jesus knows how much y'all kept me on my knees. But each of you that I prayed for and counseled on my living room couch is worth every carpet burn from being on my knees and every meal I missed when I fasted on your behalf. To God be the Glory! So let me just acknowledge some of you by name before I have to get my belt out....(*Rolls Eyes*)…LOL!!

LaKeisha Anderson, your parents raised you right. You're very loving and super respectful. To Cassandra, I believe in you! You can do this. To Mish, you'll always be my sweetie pie.

Jameka, AVP – Lord knows you kept me on my face. But you're my biggest baby. I love you. (And to the whole "Jameka original team" – WE ROCK!! We were the best – stats and all!!)

April, AVP – Ooooh you tear my nerves up!...mean self; You've made your way deep into my heart. You're closer than you know. Love you much!!!

Terrance, Terrance, Terrance, AVP – You're sooo special to me. You've been soooo respectful and have honored me on every level. You're very loving and caring. I pray God's best for your life! Countless times you have spoken a prophetic word into my spirit and was super accurate every time! I love you too.

Tawanda, AVP – OMG you give the best Sugar! What am I going to do without my good morning hugs and kisses. You're such a doll baby and so pretty. You're my baby-girl. Love you to pieces.

To Donald, Keenan, and Larry – love you guys.

To Cassius…Lord knows you're my baby and I miss you so much! I love you for life!!

Keisha, AVP; Shakee, AVP; & Miss Kim, Trainer – Love you Ladies. Much respect!! To Mr. Bobby, you're a sweetheart.

To Antonia, Senior AVP – You're a sweetheart, a jewel. God's going to use you mightily! To Sheila Slue, HR – mighty prayer warrior! Love you girlie.

PROLOGUE

"Now take your fucking clothes off so I can eat your pussy!" he said. Slowly Breeze began to reach down to remove her clothes. Her hands were shaking like a leaf. The sawed-off shotgun was pressed deep into her stomach.

"Can I lower my arms to take my pants off?" she said – her voice trembling.

"Take 'em off!" he yelled.

"But I don't want the gun to go off," she said with tears streaming down her face. He slowly released the trigger that he had pulled half way back. She reached down and pulled off her pink and white striped skinned-tight gym shorts. He slowly laid the gun down beside him never taking his eyes off of her. His eyes were cold and dark, almost as if he were in a daze with a crazed look in his eyes. She stepped out of her shorts and thong and grabbed the bottom of her wife-beater looking white tank top and began slowly pulling it over her head. More tears streamed down her face. Lord if I ever needed you it's NOW? Please don't let him kill me, Breeze prayed silently.

"Hurry the fuck up!" he yelled. If it were possible she would have jumped out of her skin. She hurriedly pulled off her tank top. He yanked her bra off and watched her as she sat on the edge of the bed. She lay back on the bed afraid to take her eyes off of him. At that moment his eyes began to change. All of a sudden the look in his eyes was the same look that always said I love you. His demeanor changed and his touch was gentle. He got on his knees in front of the bed and lifted her legs. He began licking and sucking her clit. She laid there still, her body limp. She was confused. Damn I love him, she thought. But he was crazy and she felt like he would be the death of her. Her whole body was trembling. She was terrified! He slipped his two fingers inside her warmth and started working her g-spot. She felt her buttocks begin to move to the rhythm of his tongue strokes. She gasped. Feeling her hands take on a mind of their own, she grabbed his head. She started to move her hips faster and faster while his fingers continued to stroke her g-spot.

"Ooooh...you gon'... make me...cum. Mmm...yes baby...I'm bout...to...cum"

Bam! Bam! Bam! There was a loud knock at the

door.

"What the fuck!" he said jumping up with her juices all over his face.

"Trey, Megan said she 'bout to leave yo' ass!" Breeze's cousin Jasmine yelled through the door. Breeze jumped up off the bed putting her shorts on. She grabbed her tank top putting it on wrong side out.

"I know you didn't bring that bitch to my house Trey!" Breeze screamed. "How could you?!!" She pushed past him forgetting about the gun and ran to the front door. Swinging the door open she saw the tail lights of Megan's car as she was pulling off. This bitch got some nerve, Breeze thought. I bet her ass don't know he was in here eating my pussy!

WHERE THE FUCK IS MY GUN?!!!" Trey yelled. Breeze could hear his footsteps running back towards her bedroom to get his gun. Without giving it a second thought she ran out the front door fearing for her life. She ran as fast as she could. Oh my God, which way should I go? She turned and ran to the right and made another quick right hoping he didn't see which way she ran. She darted between her house and the neighbor's house into the woods behind their backyards. She kept running as fast as she could. The sticks and sharp objects on the ground were cutting her bare feet. They started to ache against the freezing cold ground. She could feel the warm blood running out of both of her feet.

"Breeze! Stop before I shoot yo' ass!" Trey yelled.

O Jesus! She heard her own voice echoing in her head again, he's going to be the death of me. Please God don't let him catch me! Please don't let him kill me! Breeze thought loudly in her head. She kept running until she ran into some tall thick bushes. She dropped down to the ground hoping he didn't see her. She was too scared to turn around. She climbed under the thick bushes and laid there on the freezing cold ground.

BOOMP Boomp!...BOOMP Boomp!...BOOMP Boomp! Her heart was pounding hard. It pumped so hard it sounded like it was on the outside of her body. Sssshh, Breeze told her heart in fear. Please stop beating so loud, he's gonna hear you and find me. Please, please, please, she thought. She listened for his footsteps. All she could hear was her heart pounding. Oh please be quiet so I can hear if his footsteps are getting closer, she told her heart. She had never been this scared before in her entire life. She was freezing. Hot tears began to stream down her face. Her whole life began to flash before her. Without giving it a second thought, Breeze decided to make a run for it. Refusing to just lay down and take it, she got up and ran deeper into the woods and further away from her house. She ran until she came out on the other side of the neighborhood.

Exhausted, she kept running until she felt the cold asphalt under her feet. Finally she stopped and bent over to catch her breath. Her sides were hurting.

"Scccrrriiirrrkkk!!!!" Breeze looked to her left where the loud noise was coming from. Oh my God! *It was him.* She started to run straight ahead on the asphalt. Oh no, I'm making myself an easy target. He could shoot me. She made a quick right turn back into the woods. She ran and ran and ran as fast as she could. She ran until she reached the end of that set of woods. Where am I? Oh thank goodness! Breeze recognized her friend Queenie's house. Oh God please let me make it to her house before he drives around to this side of the neighborhood. She could hear a car driving fast headed her way. Oh my God! Lord please let me make it to her house! As she approached her friend's house she tried to run faster but her feet were hurting. Her heart was pounding, her chest was hurting, and her feet were still bleeding. She ran up the steps...Bam! Bam! Bam! Bam! Bam! Bam! Bam! The car was four doors down...no answer. "Pleeeaaasssee!!...she started to cry... "Open the door!!!" she yelled. The car was two houses away... right then the door opened up. She fell through the door hoping he didn't see her when he sped past her friend's house.
She slid in the house, careful not to stand up in fear that he might see her.

"Oh my God! What happened?" Queenie asked.

"Trey just tried to kill me."

CHAPTER 1

One Year Earlier

"Open the door!" Craig yelled through the door.

"No Craig, you're abusive!" Breeze yelled back. Bam! Bam! Bam!

"Open the door girl! Ain't nobody gon' bother you!"

"No! You're lying! I don't believe you!"

Silence...

"Look," he said calmly. "I haven't been here in two weeks. I'm not here to cause any trouble. All I want to do is get my clothes."

"No Craig!" You gon' hit me!"

"I promise I won't hit you baby. I know I messed up in the past but I'm not here to hurt you. I swear," he said.

Damn should I open the door or what? Maybe this time will be different and I guess I should give him his clothes, Breeze thought.

"Are you going to open the door baby?" he asked.

Silence…

"I'm serious I'm not here to start no trouble. I just need my clothes. I mean I do miss you baby but if you don't wanna be bothered with me I promise I will just get my things and leave.

Silence…she still didn't say anything.

"C'mon baby…pleeeaaase…open up." Breeze unlocked the door and cracked it open with the chain still on it. She needed to look in his eyes to see if he was telling the truth. "C'mon baby," he said through the cracked door. "I'm not gon' hurt you no more."

"You promise?"

"I promise baby. I just wanna get my clothes." Breeze closed the door and removed the chain. As soon as she turned the doorknob Craig forced the door open knocking her backwards. She stumbled and lost her balance falling to the floor. He dove on top of her and that's when she saw the sharp shiny knife.

"Move bitch and I'll stab you," he said in a calm chilling voice. Breeze laid there stricken with fear, her body stiff, careful not to move.

"You a stupid bitch. You know that?" She didn't move or say a word. He pressed the knife against her throat. "I ought'a slit your fucking throat right now." Tears began to roll down her face.

"Why are you doing this to me?"

"Bitch you belong to me! I do what the fuck I wanna do to you." He started cutting her blouse down the middle. Breeze was too scared to move. He cut her bra open and began sucking on her nipples. She felt sick. The tears kept coming.

"Please," she whimpered. "Don't do this." He didn't stop and he didn't say a word. He kept licking and sucking her nipples. Breeze felt nauseous.

"Why are you doing this to me?" He looked up and pressed the knife against the side of her throat.

"Shut the fuck up and let me do what I'm doing!" he said through his teeth while pressing the knife harder on her throat. Breeze didn't say another word. She just lay there…while he raped her.

* * *

When he got up off of her she turned to the side and laid there in a fetal position, crying. Breeze just couldn't understand why he hated her so much. What in the world did I do to deserve this? She couldn't look at Craig but she could hear him zipping his pants up. "Yeah bitch that's my pussy. And don't even think about calling the police. Cause if you do bitch I'm telling you I WILL get out of jail and I WILL come back and take your dumb ass life. And THAT'S a promise!" Breeze still didn't move or say a word. The tears kept streaming down her face. What in the world did I do to deserve this?

"When I leave lock the damn door!...stupid ass bitch!" Breeze didn't look up or move. The sound of his footsteps walking out sounded like thunder. She jumped when she heard him close the door behind himself. Breeze laid there in shock and too hurt to move. Fifteen minutes went by – she couldn't move. Thirty minutes - she was still lying there crying; asking God why this happened to her. Not able to take it any longer, forty-five minutes later Breeze grabbed her face with both her hands and began to scream.

"Yeah that's right bitch!" Craig said from outside the window. "You better scream stupid ass!" He had been watching her through the window the whole time. Somehow she found the strength to run to the door to lock it. She fumbled with the chain on the door while he banged on the door for her to let him back in. Finally she latched the chain on the door and went for her purse to get her cell phone. She ransacked her purse for her phone only to remember she had left it in her car. Besides… who was she going to tell?

CHAPTER 2

Breeze ran to her car with an arm full of clothes and threw them in the back seat. She ran back to the house, closed the door tight, locked it, put the chain on the door, and stood there panting to catch her breath. She didn't know if her heart was pounding so hard because she was out of breath or if it was because she was so scared. It was just last night that Craig had raped her and she was scared he was going to pop up out of nowhere and rape her again. Last night she'd stayed in the shower washing herself until the hot water turned cold. She scrubbed and scrubbed her skin until it burned. What am I doing? I gotta get my things out of here, she thought. She hurriedly went to her room and grabbed another armful of clothes out of the closet. She ran with them to the car and threw them in the back seat. She quickly shut the door and started running back to the house to get another armful of clothes out of the closet. She ran back to the car and threw them in the backseat. Once again she quickly shut the door and started running back to the house when...

"Breeze is that you?" Fear gripped her. She stopped in her tracks. She didn't turn around and she dared not move.

"Breeze?" the voice rang out. "What's up girl" the voice cried out. She stood there frozen in her tracks, afraid to turn around. Oh God please don't let it be him, she thought. She dared not go back in the house. He could follow me and rape me again or perhaps kill me. Oh God please!

"Breeze, what's up? It's Trey," he said. She exhaled and turned her head to look over her right shoulder.

"Oh...uh...hey," she said.

"What's wrong with you?" he asked.

"Nothing. I'm just in a hurry that's all." He was walking towards her.

"What's the rush? Hold up a minute." Oh God please make me seem normal. I can't tell anyone about what happened. Craig will kill me. When Breeze turned around, Trey was standing right in front of her.

"You look nice. Can I have a hug?"

"Sure," she said trying to sound and act normal. When he put his arms around her she started to cry.

"Hey, hey? What's wrong ma?"

"Nothing," she lied. "I just got a lot on my mind."

"C'mon now. You can trust me." He started wiping her tears. She started to cry harder.

"What's up ma?" Trey asked, concerned.

"He…raped..me!" Breeze blurted out.

"Oh shit! Who? What the…? You know what…let me help you get back to the house." He put his arm around her and walked her back to her house. She withdrew from him.

"I'm not going to hurt you. Just let me help you." Breeze wanted his help but she was afraid to trust anyone. And what if he did the same thing, she thought. They walked inside the house.

"Damn, I'm sorry that happened to you. Did you call the police?"

"No. He told me he would kill me if I did."

* * *

Skii sat in his rental car that he parked three houses down from Craig's house. He watched as Craig left his house to go to work. Like clockwork Craig was walking out the door at 7:26 am. It only took him 20 minutes to get to work and Skii knew it all too well because he had been watching him for his boy Trey for the past two weeks.

"This muthafucka…" Skii said just above a whisper as he watched Craig get into his car. It was fucked up what he had done to Breeze and now he had to pay. Knowing Craig was on his way to work, Skii pulled off and went home.

* * *

Trey didn't tell Breeze but he had planned to murk Craig for what he had done to her. He had his boy Skii laying low and watching Craig's every move. Skii had rented a different car every week so he wouldn't blow his cover. He knew where Craig worked and lived. He even knew when and where Craig went to church every Sunday.

Trey pulled his silver 2011 528i BMW into Skii's apartment complex. He took notice to the children playing in the playground area. He pulled into a parking space and got out. As he was walking up to Skii's door, the door opened before he could ring the doorbell.

"What the hell took you so long?" Skii asked Trey.

"Whaddup Skii?"

"Shit."

"You got some news for me?"

"Yeah man. This lame pussy-ass muthafucka do the same shit e'rday. He gon' be easy as hell to pop."

"Word?"

"Yeah man." Trey listened as Skii filled him in on Craig's daily routine. Together they devised a plan.

CHAPTER 3

For the next two months Trey was by Breeze's side. Although she still had some trust issues, she had begun to feel safe and comfortable with him. Breeze had reluctantly moved back into her mother's house. She hated moving back home but she had no choice, so there she was right where she'd started. She was 19 years old and needed to prove that she could make it on her own, but so much for that – for now anyway. Her mother's house was a revolving door for anyone in the family that didn't have a place to live. Her mother, known as Aunt Sadie loved her family and would do anything in her power to help anyone who needed it. She especially loved children. So here Breeze was with her younger brother and sister, Vance and Melissa, and her two younger cousins Ashley and Eva. Since the day of the rape Trey had become her protector. He had told her several times that he liked her and had liked her long before he came to her rescue that dreadful day. And if truth be told, she was feeling him too. He had attempted to make love to her twice but she wasn't ready.

"Heelllooo? Are you deaf?" Eva shouted when she opened Breeze's bedroom door.

"What?" Breeze asked agitated. "Trey is at the door for you."

"Well did anyone let him in?"

"Girl don't play dumb. You know what I meant. He's in the living room."

"Tell him I'll be out in a minute." Breeze quickly adjusted her clothes in the mirror, made sure her hair was intact and did a quick breath test.

"Heeey," her voice sang as she approached the living room. "How are you today?"

"I'm good. Just coming by to check on you. You good?"

"Yeah…a little bored though."

"Well I'm on the way home. If you want, you can come with me to my house. We could maybe watch a Kevin Hart DVD – something to make you laugh."

"That sounds great. I'd love to."

"Cool. I'll order pizza when we get there. That cool?"

"Sure."

When they got to Trey's house Breeze marveled at his set up. He had taste. His living room furniture was nice rich chocolate brown leather accented with wooden and glass end tables. The lamps on the end tables added much flavor.

"You can have a seat," Trey said. She sat on the couch. Trey put the DVD in and left her in the living room alone while he went to shower and change his clothes.

Kevin Hart was saying, "Say it wit'cha chest," when Trey came back into the living room. He had ordered pizza while he was in his room.

"You good?" he asked her.

"Yeah I'm good."

"You want something to drink?" Right then the doorbell rang. It was the pizza being delivered. Trey answered the door and paid the gentleman for the pizza. He took it into the kitchen and brought Breeze a glass of lemonade. When she looked up at him, he sat the glass of lemonade on the end table and leaned down to kiss her. He must've been feeling her because she was beginning to want him for the first time but she purposely did not make the first move. When he noticed she wasn't resisting him like the times before he parted her lips with his tongue and slipped it into her mouth. He placed both his hands on her face and continued kissing her and gently biting her bottom lip. She wondered what he was like. He continued to kiss her passionately. He was a great kisser if she must say so herself. He kissed her neck. Breeze leaned her head over to the side welcoming his gentle kisses. He was making her love box wet. Her nipples were already hard when he pulled both of her breasts out of her blouse. He began lightly licking, sucking, and biting on them softly. She felt her middle getting hotter. He bent down on his knees and slid her shorts and panties off...she didn't stop him. He pulled her hips to the edge of the couch. She watched him with desire as he lifted her legs up over his shoulders. He began licking her pussy and sucking her pearl until she came. He slipped his love muscle out and began massaging her pussy with it making it wetter. Catching her off guard he thrust the head of his thick shaft into her hot love box.

"What the hell?" she asked as she jerked her hips away from him.

"Relax," he said.

"You hurt me."

"C'mere," he said gently pulling her ass back to all nine inches of his dick. "I'll be easy baby…just relax." He slowly entered her again. "Take a deep breath." She inhaled and he slid more of his thick long shaft inside her. She closed her eyes tight and clinched her nails into his back.

"That's it baby. Take it," he whispered in her ear.

"I can't. It's too much," she said looking into his eyes. He kissed her as he slowly slid more of his humongous dick deeper and deeper into her warmth. All she could do was moan with pleasure…and take it. He slid his dick in and out of her until her walls gave way and began to fit him like a glove. She held him tight.

"Damn this pussy wet….shit!….I'm bout….to cum…. Cum on wit' me baby." She looked in his eyes while he grinded the bottom of her pussy. She rolled her ass round and round in harmony with him. He began again to slide in and out of her until they exploded together.

CHAPTER 4

"Auntie is it okay if I stay here for a little while? Me and my mama just had a huge fight again and I'm just tired of her drug habits!" Breeze's cousin Jasmine began to cry as she was telling Aunt Sadie what happened between her and her mother. Jasmine's mother was Aunt Sadie's baby sister – Desa Rae. She had been on crack for the past 12 years and Jasmine just couldn't take it anymore.

"Sure baby. We can put another twin bed in the room with the other set of bunk beds." Aunt Sadie told her. Sighing with relief, Jasmine got up and went out to the car where her boyfriend Tariq was waiting with her already packed bags.

"Can you help me take my bags in the house? My

aunt said yes. I told you she would." Tariq didn't respond as he got out of the car to help his girlfriend get her things out of the car. Something about this move just didn't sit well with him.

"Hey girl. What'chu doing here?" Breeze asked Jasmine.

"Aunt Sadie said I could stay here for a while. My mama's been up to her same ol' same ol'."

"Oh. Okay...wow."

"Maybe now I can get some peace of mind."

"True. I hope she gets it together."

"So what's up girl? What'chu got going on tonight?"

"Nothing. I'm probably just gon' chill with my friend."

"Ooooh," Jasmine sang. "You looking all giddy and shit. Let me find out you in love."

"I don't know about all that, but I do like him though – a lot. He's cool. Girl how-bout this...he told me he's been digging me for a long time. And I didn't even know it. I guess I was too busy being all into Craig."

"Oh yeah! What happened with you and Craig anyway? Y'all ain't together no more?"

"Girrrlll no!"

"What happened?"

"Chile I don't even want to talk about it. It was a bad break up. But my friend sort of stepped in and rescued me."

"Okaaay. Alright. I hear ya. So he was on some ol' Zorro shit." They both laughed.

"So what's up with you?" Breeze asked changing the subject.

"Nothing much. Just need peace of mind. Tired of the drama with my mama on n'em drugs I just couldn't take it anymore. So I asked Auntie if I could stay here."

"Well you know we're all here for you. Gimme a hug."

"Breeeezzee!" your friend is at the door for you!" Eva shouted from the living room.

"Oh shit, girl that's him." Breeze told Jasmine while blushing. "Come on in the living room with me so you can meet him."

***

"Jasmine this is my friend Trey. Trey this is my cousin Jasmine." Trey and Jasmine stared at each other as if they had just seen a ghost.

"What?" Breeze asked. "Y'all know each other or something?"

"Yeah..."

"No..." Trey said interrupting Jasmine.

"I mean I met him a couple of months ago when I was over here visiting, Jasmine explained."

"Here at the house?" Breeze asked.

"No silly. I met him at the community store." Breeze made a mental note that Trey was letting Jasmine tell the story of how they met without interrupting her or adding to the story.

"Damn girl why didn't you tell me?" Breeze asked.

"Cause it wasn't shit."

"O a'ight. I hear ya..."

"So what's up baby? You chillin with me or what?" Trey asked interrupting them.

"Absolutely." Breeze said while getting her purse. " I am sooo ready to get out of this house."

* * *

Ring! Ring! Ring! Ring! Ring! Ring!

"Shit! Answer the goddamn phone!" frantic Jasmine said aloud as she paced the floor back and forth waiting for her friend Sheree to answer the phone.

"Hel-lo."

"Damn bitch what took you so long to answer the phone?"

"I was in the shower bitch. And this better be important cause I done got my ass out the shower to answer the phone. You been blowin' me up like crazy."

"I know. I know. But check this out...remember my cousin Breeze? Girl she is fucking with that dude Trey I told you about."

"Who the fuck is that?"

"Bitch don't play dumb. You know, the dude I told you I fucked with the big ass dick!"

"Oh shit! Stop lying!"

"I swear to god."

"What the hell you gon' do? You gon' tell her you fucked him?"

"Hell no! I ain't seen my cousin this happy in a long ass time. But when she introduced us I thought I was gon' shit bricks."

"Damn!"

"I know right?"

"I wish I would'a been a fly on the wall so I could'a seen yo' ass. I bet that shit was funny as hell."

"Fuck you bitch. That shit wasn't funny. I didn't know what the hell to do."

"Ain't shit to do. Hell all you did was fuck the nigga."

"Yeah a few times. But I swear that nigga was looking fine as hell tonight."

"Well you said you wasn't gone tell your cousin and besides you said she's happy so you might as well put that shit out yo' damn mind."

"Damn...and I fucked that nigga raw too."

"Daaayyyuumm bitch!"

CHAPTER 5

Breeze gripped the sheets with both hands while Trey sucked her clit and licked her pussy from behind.

"Baby you gotta stop," Breeze moaned while trying to pull away from him.

"Never baby. Not until you cum." He locked his arms around both her legs and pulled her ass back to his mouth. Her body shivered from the sensitivity of him making her cum so hard.

"Please baby...let me go...you driving me crazy!"

"I'm not done yet," he said seductively. He sucked and licked all the juices from her love box. Then switching positions, he laid on his back and she took him into her mouth, making it super wet, and sucked his love muscle like a lollipop. His toes started to curl when she began to deep throat him. Just when she heard him start to breath heavily she turned around and mounted his long thick shaft backwards in the bicycle position. She slid down on his thick nine inches slowly. Once she got it all in she began to grind causing his dick to bang against the bottom of her pussy. Breeze began to moan with painful pleasure.

"Oooo…you gon' make me cum again," she said.

"Cum with me ma." She leaned forward and grabbed both his ankles. She glided up and down his fat long pole squeezing her pussy walls each time she raised up off his dick. She opened up her pussy as she slid down on it. When she got it all in again she gripped her pussy tight and continued to squeeze it until she reached the top of it, glided down on it and did it over and over until they came together. When he was done exploding inside her she once again squeezed her pussy tight raising up off his dick taking in all of his love juice.

"Damn ma you a beast with that shit," Trey said exhausted.

"All for you daddy," she said climbing up beside him and lying her head on his chest. He placed his arms around her and pulled her closer.

"I love you," he said.

"I...I..."

"Shhh. Don't say anything," he said. "Just relax," he said kissing her forehead. "Let's go to sleep."

She decided to do as he said and kept quiet. She relaxed in his arms and they fell asleep.

Breeze woke up the next morning to find that she was in bed alone. She got up and went over to her bedroom window. Trey's car was gone. She smiled lightly and shifted her head back slightly with her arms folded as she reminisced about him telling her he loves her. Damn I love his swag, she thought. She turned around to go into the kitchen to make her some breakfast. Suddenly she felt like she was starving. She went over to her dresser to throw on a pair of shorts and a t-shirt. That's when she saw the note...

> *You were sleeping so good I didn't want to wake you. Had some business to take care of. I'll come see you when I'm done. And don't think too hard about what I said last night – believe it.*

CHAPTER 6

It had been one week and Breeze still hadn't seen or heard from Trey. Her phone calls were still going straight to voicemail when she dialed his cell. That wasn't like him so she wasn't sure if something was wrong or if he was regretting telling her he loves her. She looked over at her digital clock. It's bright red numbers displayed 11:32 pm. Where the hell is he? Maybe he doesn't love me after all. I knew I shouldn't have fucked with him like that. Shoud'a never gave him the cookie. Damn was he playing with me all along just to get the pussy? I could kick my own ass. She knew a week wasn't really a long time but he had never stayed away from her that long. In fact they had been together every day since he rescued her from Craig. She began to cry as she regretted ever getting involved with him. And before she knew it she had drifted off to sleep.

Tap! Tap! Tap! Breeze jumped as the annoying sound awakened her from her sleep.

Tap! Tap! Tap! The bright red digits on her alarm clock displayed the time once again, 2:02 am.

"Who's there?"

"It's me, Trey. Come open the door and let me in." Reluctantly she went to the front door and opened it with an attitude.

"Why are you at my window at 2 am in the damn morning?"

"Right now ma I don't need your attitude. I need to talk to you," he said brushing past her. Locking the door she followed him into her room. He quickly undressed and got into her bed. Breeze stood there looking at him. He had some damn nerve! Part of her was glad he was there and the other part of her was blazing because she hadn't heard from him. She didn't get in bed too quickly because she didn't want to seem too anxious. Trey reached his hand out to her inviting her into her own bed. Breeze stood there looking at him like he had a serious problem.

"Don't be like that ma," he pleaded. She dropped her folded arms, sucked her teeth and rolled her eyes as she walked over to him. She sat down harshly on the edge of the bed.

"C'mere," he said gently pulling her arm to lie beside him. She lay down in bed turning her back to him, careful not to let him touch her. Trey grabbed her arm and pulled up to her bumper causing his dick to rest against her ass. Damn. What the fuck! she thought. He was breaking her that quick. She felt his warmth against her skin. Damn he felt good.

"I'm sorry ma." Breeze dared not say anything.

"I know I fucked up," he said kissing the back of her neck. She sucked her teeth as if to seem uninterested, still not saying a word. "You forgive me?" She still said nothing but shook her head yes. Silence fell between them. Trey was still holding her tight when she looked at her digital clock once again. It's big bright red numbers didn't disappoint her this time either as it silently screamed the time. 3:13 am.

"I killed somebody tonight."

"What the...?" she said while trying to pull away from him. He locked his grip on her so that she couldn't move.

"Don't run from me. I need you ma." She didn't know what to say or how to feel.

"I...uh..."

"Shhh...don't talk...just listen," he whispered. And that is when the confessions of the gangster she loved began....

* * *

It was Sunday morning and once again Skii had followed Craig to church. Skii was still waiting for him to come out when he picked up the phone to call Trey.

Ring! Ring! Still in bed with Breeze, Trey reached over her to answer his phone.

"Yo'," he said still groggy from being awakened out of his sleep.

"Get yo' ass up nigga!" Skii shouted into the phone.

"Whaddup?" Trey said still sounding sleepy."

"Meet me at my pad at 3 o'clock."

"A'ight fam."

"One." They hung up.

Still holding Breeze in one arm, Trey placed his other hand on her arm and turned her towards him and kissed her forehead. She snuggled up to him laying her head on his chest.

"Listen to me," he said rubbing her head. "I have to leave again to handle some more business. She gasped and started to feel nervous for his safety.

"Don't worry ma. I'll be fine. I promise I'm coming back to you."

"When?" she asked – fear filling her voice.

"Soon. But before I go I want you to promise me one thing."

"What is it baby?"

"What we have is solid, right?"

"Yeeaahh," she said not sure where he was taking the conversation.

"Then promise me you'll always tell me the truth no matter what. And I promise to always tell you the truth – no matter what. That's how we will keep the foundation of our relationship solid and strong. That way baby, we will last forever."

"Sure baby. No problem, I promise."

"And one more thing."

"What's that?"

"No matter what, promise me you'll never leave me," he said looking into her eyes.

"Baby that's two things, you said one," she said jokingly. He didn't smile to acknowledge her humor. He kept a serious face while still looking into her eyes. She knew then he was serious.

"Okay baby, I promise," she said sealing it with a kiss.

CHAPTER 7

"I'm pregnant."

"Are you serious?" Tariq asked Jasmine.

"No, I'm lying for my health," Jasmine answered sarcastically. "Of course I'm serious."

"Damn baby you just made me the happiest man alive." Tariq picked her up and spinned her around. "So now I've got to speed up the process. Gotta hurry up and get us a place."

"That's right, you do. I can't stay at Aunt Sadie's place forever."

"So how far along are you?"

"Does it matter?"

"Of course it matters. Everything about my son matters."

"Son?"

"That's right, my son."

"Whatever...I say it's a girl."

"Forget about it. That's my son in there," Tariq said kissing her stomach. Jasmine didn't have the heart to tell Tariq that it wasn't his baby. She was actually three months pregnant with Trey's baby. She had it all figured out in her mind. She was three months pregnant but she would tell Tariq she was only six weeks and when it was time to deliver the baby she would tell him the baby was premature.

"And I want him to have my full name: Tariq Andre' Williams," Tariq said sternly. Jasmine slipped off into a daze and began to reminisce about the day she met Trey. She was walking out of the community convenient store. Trey was driving by slowly in his silver BMW with his shiny new rims making a statement. Damn who the fuck is that? he thought. Jasmine was rocking a short Mohawk haircut. Her French manicure was neatly done. She sported her cream colored Gucci short set and gold Gucci sandals. Looking fly as ever she stepped onto the pavement with confidence. Trey hit the automatic button to roll his window down.

"Whaddup Ma?" Trey asked Jasmine.

"Shit," Jasmine answered.

"You tryn'a go have dinner with me?"

"I'on know you."

"That's why I'm gon' take you to dinner," he said with a smile – not giving Jasmine the option to say no. "We gon' get to know each other over dinner."

"How you figure you got it like that?"

"Cause I do Ma. So what's up?"

"Whatev…"

"Stop playing hard to get."

"I'm not playing hard to get. It is what it is."

"So what's up? Where we going to eat?"

"Shit I'on know. You tell me."

"A'ight Ma get in – dinner's waiting." Jasmine

walked around the front of the car letting him watch her switch her ass hard and got in the car on the passenger side.

"So what's your name?" Trey asked pulling out of the parking lot.

* * *

Bang! Bang! Bang! Bang! Bang! Bang! Bang! That was the headboard banging against the wall of the hotel room as Trey pounded his dick in and out of Jasmine. He had taken her to Red Lobster, her favorite place to eat, for dinner. When she chose Red Lobster Trey knew getting that pussy would be a piece of cake. He had predetermined she would be an easy lay. Women are so predictable, he thought. He pounded harder and harder until he unloaded inside of her. He lowered her legs from the buck position he had her in and fell over on top of her.

"I'on usually do this," Jasmine said just above a whisper in Trey's ear.

"Do what Ma?"

"Give it up on the first date."

"Don't worry Ma, it's all good."

"I just don't want you to think I'ma hoe."

"Yo' Ma, chill. I ain't even thinking like that," Trey

lied.

The next morning when Trey woke up he urged Jasmine to turn over on her stomach so he could hit it from behind relieving himself of his morning hard-on. Three hours later he was dropping her off at her best friend's house.

"A'ight Ma I'ma get at you later."

"Okay. Make sure you do," Jasmine said with a smile.

"That's what's up," Trey said hitting the automatic button to roll up his window.

* * *

"Jasmine! Tariq yelled snapping Jasmine out of her daze. Jasmine jumped.

"Damn! You scared me."

"Shit you act like you was in a trance or something."

"Oh I was just imagining what it will be like when the baby is born."

"It's gon' be all good."

"I know. I can't wait till you get us a place."

"Oh for sho' baby. That's coming real soon."

"Can you make it fast please?"

"Don't worry baby. I'ma make it happen," Tariq said softly kissing her lips.

* * *

Tariq was elated that he was going to be a father. He had wanted a son for quite some time and he didn't care what Jasmine said, he knew he was having a son. A big grin swept across his face. Yeah I'ma have a mini me running around. Can't wait for that shit. Tariq's thoughts led him to think about his girl. He continued to smile, proud that he had pulled someone that fine. But hell he wasn't no slouch himself he thought. Rubbing his clean shaven caramel-colored face. Tariq wore a low cut faded hair cut with deep waves. His hazel eyes and pretty white teeth always caught the ladies attention along with his washboard abs.

Tariq had been working part-time at UPS. It had been enough for him only because he had been living at home with his parents. Now that he was dating Jasmine he needed more money. He needed to be able to take her to her favorite restaurant Red Lobster whenever she wanted, take her to the movies, buy her drinks at the club whenever they went, and keep her hair and nails and feet done. That being the case he sold bootleg DVD's, but now that they were going to have a son even that hustle was no longer enough. He knew he needed to get a place for Jasmine before the baby was born. He wanted to fully furnish the pad with all that she and the baby needed before the baby boy was born. He had to think of something and he had to think fast. He had told Jasmine he was going to make it happen and that's exactly what he'd planned to do.

CHAPTER 8

"Sorry Mr. Williams but we are going to have to let you go. Right now we're over-staffed and need to cut back on the number of employees we have on board. But the good news is you'll be first on the list to call when we start hiring again for the Christmas rush," exclaimed Tariq's supervisor. Damn, Tariq thought. He didn't need this shit right now, especially with the new baby coming soon. He would just have to get a new job. But this time it would have to be full time. He was determined to do the right thing by Jasmine and his son.

* * *

Ring! Ring! Ring! Jasmine ran to the phone. She had been expecting to hear from Tariq all day.

"Hello?" she spoke into the receiver.

"Yo, whaddup? Breeze there?"

"Who dis?"

"This Trey."

"Oh Trey what's up? This is Jasmine. I been waiting to talk to you."

"About what?"

"I need to tell you something."

"Whaddup?"

"I'm pregnant."

"Fuck you telling me for?"

"Because it's yours!" Jasmine said with an attitude.

"That ain't none of my muthafuckin kid! Bitch you trippin'!"

"It is yours! It ain't like you didn't fuck me raw!"

"No fuck it ain't either. Bitch put Breeze on the phone!"

"Fuck you!"

"Fuck you – ho!'

"You wasn't saying that three months ago when you was fucking me!" Jasmine shot back.

"Bitch put Breeze on the phone!"

"You better be glad I love my cousin or else I would tell her I'm pregnant by your sorry ass!"

"I don't give a fuck!"

"We'll see when she finds out about your baby!" Jasmine stated sarcastically.

"And you'll make me fuck yo' ass up too!"

"I wish you would put your dirty ass hands on me! I'll have my people murk yo ass!"

"Bitch miss me with all that bullshit. I ain't got time for this stupid ass shit! Put Breeze on the phone!!" he shouted getting more frustrated.

"She ain't here dumbass! Click! Jasmine slammed the phone on the receiver.

Eva was careful to wait until both Trey and Jasmine hung up both their phones. She didn't want either one of them to know she had been ear-hustling their conversation the whole time. She finally eased the other phone in her bedroom down on the receiver. She could hardly believe her own ears. Instantly she hated she didn't hang the phone up at the very beginning of the conversation. Now she had to decide whether or not she would be the bearer of bad news or pretend as if she'd heard nothing at all. She sighed. Decisions, decisions, decisions, she thought while shaking her head.

CHAPTER 9

Skii pulled into Trey's driveway and honked the horn. He had promised Trey a month ago he would drive him to court just in case he got locked up this time. Trey's case had gotten postponed twice before and his lawyer had informed him that he was going to ask for a continuance once again since Trey had paid him such a hefty amount to do so.

Hooonk! Hooonk! Skii laid on the horn again. Man why the hell this muthafucka ain't ready? Damn! He gon' be late for his own damn funeral. Just then Trey opened his front door and headed towards the car.

"Bout damn time nigga!" Skii said.

"Good the fuck morning to you too!" They sped off headed to downtown Charlotte where the courthouse is located on Fourth Street. On the way down there they talked shit about a whole lot of nothing and little bit of everything.

"So when you gon' tell your girl about this court case?" Skii asked Trey.

"Shit man I don't wanna tell her. But I plan on taking her to dinner tonight and telling her then."

"Tonight?" Man yo' ass might not even see her tonight. They might lock yo ass up today. You should have told her before now."

"Shit man I know. I just didn't have the heart to tell her. I didn't want to hurt her. She's been through enough as it is."

"So what if you get locked up today?"

"Then I guess you'll have to tell her."

"That's fucked up, you know that right?"

"It would be fucked up if I was going to jail today, but I'm not nigga."

"How the fuck you know?"

"Cause nigga I ain't paying this muthafuckin'

lawyer all this paper for nothing.

* * *

Trey and Breeze had finished their steak dinner at Chima Brazilian Steakhouse in the heart of downtown Charlotte. They were both sipping on a glass of wine while waiting for their dessert. Breeze had noticed Trey was somewhat quiet and didn't talk as much as he usually does.

"I have something I need to tell you baby," Trey said.

"Okay baby. What's up?" Breeze said giving him her undivided attention.

"I gotta go away for a while."

"What do you mean?" she said with a puzzled look on her face.

"I gotta go make some time." She dropped her head in disappointment.

Trey lifted her chin with his forefinger. "Don't look like that ma. You breaking my heart."

"How long have you known this, Trey?"

"For a while now."

"What am I supposed to do?" He didn't respond.

"Why, Trey?! Why didn't you tell me?"

"I didn't want to hurt you!"

"You didn't want to hurt me? Well what do you think you've done now?!!"

"I'm sorry ma. I should've told you sooner," he said softening his voice.

"I can't believe you!" She stood up from her seat. Her pain suddenly turned to anger. She couldn't believe he would lead her to think all is well when he knew all along he would be leaving her. "You should'a just left me alone!" My life would've been fine without you!"

"I..."

"Save it! I don't want to hear it!" She turned and headed to the door to leave.

"Breeze wait!" She ignored him and kept walking. When she got outside she flagged a taxi. A Yellow Cab pulled over to the right side of the curb. She opened the back door and got in. "To Hyde Park please," she instructed. Just when she was closing the door, Trey opened the door and slid in the backseat forcing her to move over.

"What the hell are you doing?"

"Man take us to the Courtyard Marriott on W.T.

Harris," Trey instructed the taxi driver.

"I don't wanna go with you!"

"I don't give a fuck! You going where the fuck I say you going!" Breeze turned around and slapped him as hard as she could. He quickly grabbed her hand and twisted it behind her back, pulling her towards him causing her back and arm to lean against his chest.

"Let me go!" she screamed.

"Not till you calm down." He grabbed her other hand and placed it behind her back too.

"LET ME GO!" she screamed again.

"You gon' calm down?"

"LET ME GO TREY!" She wiggled and tried to get herself loose. He continued to hold her, not saying a word. She sat there breathing hard, her chest rising and falling rapidly.

"Everything alright back there?" the taxi driver asked.

"**Mind your business**!" they both shouted simultaneously.

"Man I got this back here. You just get us to the hotel," Trey said. Breeze yanked herself hard trying to break away from his grip – to no avail.

"Not till you calm down ma," Trey said in a calm voice.

She jerked again trying to free herself. "I don't want to be with you right now!"

"You ain't got no choice. Whether you like it or not, I'm not going anywhere."

"Arrgghh!!" she screamed.

"Calm the fuck down!"

"Leave me alone!"

"Calm down!" he said pulling her hands tighter behind her back.

"You're hurting me!"

"Well calm down!" he said not releasing his grip.

"Okay I'm calm!" Breeze said feeling defeated.

"When you really calm down I'll let you go." Neither one of them said anything for the next 10 minutes. The taxi driver kept driving.

"Let me say this to you," Trey finally said. "When we get to the hotel I'ma let you go. I'm not going to do anything to you. Just come up to the room with me and let me explain. After that, if you still want to leave I promise I won't stop you." She didn't say anything. The taxi driver pulled into the Courtyard Marriott Hotel circling around to the front entrance. After paying the taxi fare they got out of the car and walked through the hotel lobby to the room he had reserved earlier that day. He had planned to take her there after dinner. When he unlocked the door she walked into the room with much attitude. When he turned around to face her after locking the door and placing the do not disturb sign on the outside of the door, she slapped him again. She raised her hand to slap him again, but this time he caught her hand in midair.

"That was your last time slapping me. I'm telling you, you better chill with that shit!"

"You lied to me!" she yelled. Once he let her hands go she started wildly beating his chest with her fists.

"I hate you!" she said.

"You don't mean that!" he shot back.

"Yes I do! I hate you! I hate you! I hate you!" she yelled. Before she knew it he swooped down, picked her up and carried her over to the bed. He fell over on the bed with her underneath him. He straddled her and grabbed both her hands locking his hands within hers.

"I didn't lie to you ma."

"You did!"

"Please baby, just hear me out." She lay still, softening up a little. "After all you've been through I just didn't have the heart to tell you. All I wanted to do is protect you and be there for you."

"Well now you're not going to be here!"

"You think this shit don't hurt me too!" She didn't say anything. Tears filled his eyes. "A year ago I shot somebody and he didn't die. He remembered my face and pointed me out in a line-up. That's how they got me. I was charged with assault with a deadly weapon with intent to kill. Since then I've been in and out of court. That's where I was this morning."

"I trusted you," she said tears rolling down the sides of her face.

"And you *can* still trust me baby."

"You promised we would always tell each other the truth no matter what."

"And baby that's what I'm doing now." She turned her head and let her tears continue to fall. "I love you, he said, kissing her tears. Breeze could feel his love muscle getting hard. He moved one of his hands and unzipped his pants and released himself. Breeze didn't stop him. He lifted her dress and slid her thong to the side. With his other hand he thrust the head of his swollen shaft inside her.

She gasped and by quick reflexes her arms embraced him with force.

"I love you baby," he said pushing himself deeper inside her. Her tears continued to flow.

"I'm scared baby."

"Sh-h-h, I gotchu baby," he whispered in her ear. She held him tight. Just promise you won't ever leave me baby."

"I promise baby," she said. He caressed her and grinded his dick slowly, making her feel all of him. Damn he makes it hurt so good, she thought. They continued to make love in harmony until they both came, causing Breeze, for the moment, to forget about the issue at hand.

CHAPTER 10

"Fuck man!" Tariq exclaimed as he swept the papers off his mother's dining room table. He felt as if he was down on his luck. He had a new baby on the way and had recently lost his job at UPS. He heard his boss's voice replay in his head, *But the good news is you'll be one of the first on the list to call when we start hiring for the Christmas rush.* Well that wasn't going to work for Tariq.

"How the fuck am I supposed to tell Jasmine this shit?!!" he yelled. He grabbed his head with both his hands and paced the floor back and forth. She was depending on him to get a new pad for her and the baby. His heart wouldn't let him disappoint her. There was only one thing left to do. He picked up his cell phone and dialed the number he had saved in his phone just in case he ever needed it. The phone rang four times before someone answered.

"Hello?"

"Whaddup fam?" Tariq asked.

"Yo, who dis?"

"Tariq, man. Whaddup wit'cha?"

"Shit."

"Yo, you still wanna do that lick?"

* * *

Eva could hear Breeze's footsteps as she headed to the dining room after fixing her plate. Sunday was the only day of the week that Breeze's mom, Aunt Sadie cooked and today was no exception. She had baked a turkey ham, made her famous potato salad, green beans seasoned with smoked turkey, squash casserole, cornbread, and homemade lemonade. And Breeze could hardly wait to sit down and start eating. But to Eva, Breeze's footsteps sounded like thunder as she was walking to the table. To Eva's ears the rest of the room was still and stiff with silence. All she could hear was those thunder-like footsteps.

"What the hell is wrong with you girl?" Aunt Sadie yelled at Eva causing her to jump, breaking her trance. "Didn't you hear me talking to you?"

"I heard you!" Eva shouted back with an attitude.

"Ain't nothing wrong with her. She just needs to get some rest," Ashley said trying to keep Eva from blurting out Jasmine and Trey's juicy little secret. Knowing Ashley wouldn't breathe a word, Eva told her what she had found out.

"I don't need no damn rest. I feel fine!" Eva said with attitude. "You don't need to be trying to figure out what's going on with me. You need to be asking Breeze what's going on with her man."

"Eva what are you talking about? It's always some shit wit'chu!" Breeze shot back.

"Ain't shit with me bitch! You need to check your man!"

"Oh here we go!" What is the problem now? Why can't you just be happy for me for a damn change? Ever since we were little, you always had it in for me!"

"Whatever! You too damn gullible to see the truth."

"What are you talking about? If you got something to say, say it!"

"The food is getting cold," Ashley nervously

interjected.

"That's right," Aunt Sadie added, nervous about what Eva might say. "C'mon let's finish eating."

"No! Let her say what she gotta say! Let's settle this shit now!" Breeze said.

"You couldn't handle the truth if I told yo' dumb ass!"

In what seemed like a millisecond Breeze jumped across the table and charged at Eva grabbing her neck with both hands. Eva fell backwards as Breeze landed on top of her. Eva grabbed Breeze's hands trying to loosen her grip. Aunt Sadie and Ashley tried pulling Breeze off of Eva. But Breeze was beyond anger and wouldn't let go. Eva's eyes began to roll to the back of her head due to lack of oxygen. Both Ashley and Aunt Sadie were screaming "Let her go!" while still trying to pull Breeze off of Eva. Clenching her teeth Breeze had tuned everything out around her. She suddenly heard a small still voice that said, *"Don't do it."* Sensing it was the voice of God Breeze let Eva go. Eva quickly grabbed her neck and started gasping for air.

While her mother and Ashley were holding her back she shot an evil look at Eva and said, "I'm sick of you!" Stay the hell away from me and outta my damn business!"

"That's how stupid you are bitch! You so damn

blind you can't see the fucking forest for the trees! You open your damn eyes you might get a fucking clue that Jasmine is pregnant by ya man – Trey!"

Eva's words stung Breeze. It felt like pins and needles hit her in the face. She stood there speechless and in shock. She couldn't believe what she had just heard.

CHAPTER 11

Craig woke up with a black satin pillow case over his head, tied tight around his neck. His hands were tied tight behind his back with wire. His wrists were cut and bleeding from the tightness of the wires. His feet were bound and taped together with gray duct tape to the bottom of the chair he was sitting in. Immediately he was stricken with fear and didn't know what had happened to him and he certainly didn't know how he had gotten where he was. Every part of his body ached. It was clear to him he had been beaten. He could taste his own blood in his mouth. His head was aching, clearly he had taken many blows to the head. As he tried to remember how he had gotten there he suddenly felt ice cold water being poured over his head. He wanted to ask questions or perhaps even scream but his mouth was also taped with gray duct tape.

The freezing water woke Craig up even more. His body trembled all over partly due to fear, the other because of the freezing cold water. His mind raced as he tried to remember what in the hell he had done to deserve this. He'd been going to church every Sunday so he could not figure out for the life of him why he had been so brutally beaten. Right then he felt a harsh blow to the left side of his head. He began to piss on himself.

"You woke now muthafucka?" Skii yelled. Craig tried to identify Skii's voice but soon realized he'd never heard his voice before. Skii hit him again.

"Wondering why you here muthafucka? Huh?" Whack!! Skii hit him again. He knew Craig couldn't speak, after all he'd been the one that tied him up.

"You sorry piece of shit," Skii disdainfully said to Craig, "I wanna put a bullet in your head so fucking bad. But I get to keep whooping your ass till my man gets here. I'll let him have the honor of putting your fucking lights out, you worthless piece of shit!"

Craig still couldn't figure it out. He began to think of all the bad things he'd recently done. He never once thought about what he'd done to Breeze. He had been going to church but he had never repented for what he had done. He only went because he felt that as long as he went to church every Sunday it would justify all his sins. As he searched his mind, he thought surely he was being treated this way because just one week ago he had beaten his girl Jessica and had had sex with her against her will. If he were not tied up he would kick his own ass for not scaring her enough not to open her big ass mouth.

Now here he was sitting here being beaten, probably by some of her family members. Should've killed that bitch, he thought as he sat there in pain while Skii continued to torture him until Trey arrived.

* * *

You've reached the voicemail for Breeze McKnight. At the moment I am unavailable to take your call. At the sound of the tone, please leave a brief message and as soon as I'm available I will return you call. **Beeeep!!**

"Baby dis Trey. I don't know what's up or why you ain't returning my phone calls. This ain't like you baby. Call me back. Let me know what's up." He pressed the talk button to end the call for the 37th time. It had been two weeks since he'd seen or talked to Breeze. Each time he called it seemed as if she was sending his calls to voicemail on purpose. He thought for sure the last time they were together everything was okay. He just couldn't figure it out. They had talked things over and she seemed to be fine. He just knew for sure they were back on good terms, especially after passionately making love that Thursday night. On the way to her house she had told him she was excited about having Sunday dinner with her family. When she got out of the car she kissed him and told him she would call him later. Something just wasn't right. She had never gone this long without calling him or returning his calls. He purposed in his mind that he would go over there as soon as he took care of Craig who was being held hostage by his boy Skii in an abandoned warehouse on 36th Street.

* * *

Trey walked into the warehouse and down the stairs into the basement where Skii was holding Craig.

"Fuck is you tremblin' for...bitch ass nigga?" Trey yelled at Craig. Once again Craig tried to place the voice. He didn't recognize this one either.

"Gon' make you pay for what you did to my girl!" Trey said hitting Craig with the butt of his pistol. Craig still had no clue who Trey was talking about.

"Just so you know muthafucka I had my man to follow yo' sorry ass for the past few months!" Now it's time to pay!" Craig shrugged his shoulders like he didn't know what Trey was talking about.

"Oh you don't know what I'm talking about? Remember Breeze muthafucka?" Craig dropped his head knowing he was doomed. "Now it's time to pay," Trey said putting a bullet through Craig's head killing him instantly. "Clean this lousy piece of shit up and don't leave no trace," Trey said to Skii as he was walking back up the stairs to leave. And no one ever heard anything of Craig ever again.

CHAPTER 12

Tariq sped down Sunset Road headed towards Beatties Ford Road watching the flashing blue lights in the rearview and side view mirrors. He was leading CMPD (Charlotte Mecklenburg Police Department) in a high speed chase. Driving at 90 mph he darted in and out of traffic and in between cars trying not to cause an accident. As his heart raced with fear he began to regret what he had just done.

Tariq and his partner Black walked into a fast-food restaurant on Sunset Road, their heads covered with black toboggan masks.

"Everybody get on the floor now!" Black yelled

as he waived his 45 pistol. Frantically customers and employees got down on the floor afraid for their lives. At the same time the manager secretly pressed the silent button under the counter to alert the police. Black pointed the gun at the manager.

"You!" he said, "Lead me to the safe!"

A woman who was under a table with her four year old daughter slowly reached for her cell phone. Her fingers were trembling as she started dialing 911. Before she could dial the last number Tariq placed the 9 mm pistol to her head and demanded her to give him the phone. She nervously handed him her phone with tears rolling down her face. She grabbed her little girl who was stricken with shock and pulled her closer to her and held her tightly. Tariq looked directly into her eyes and said, "Make another move like that and I'll blow your fucking brains out!"

In the back of the restaurant Black was pistol whipping the manager who did not know the combination to the safe.

"Yo!" Tariq yelled from the dining room. "Hurry up man. We gotta move!! I hear sirens!!" Black hit the manager with the butt of his pistol one last time. "Today's your lucky day muthafucka!" he said shoving the manager into the freezer locking him in. Black tried opening the safe himself one last time. "Shit!" he said unable to figure out the combination.

"Yo Black, hurry up man! They gettin' closer!!!"

Approaching the dining room Black drew the gun on his friend, "Muthafucka did you just say my name in front of all these witnesses?"

"Oh shit man! I wasn't thinking!"

"You wasn't thinking?" What the fuck?!!!" Black said getting ready to pull the trigger. When Tariq noticed Black was really going to shoot him he pulled the trigger first killing Black instantly with one single gunshot to the head. He then turned and ran out the door to the getaway vehicle, a black Ford Mustang. He escaped right as the police were arriving. He jumped in the car and sped off onto Sunset Road.

Tariq's cell phone rang snapping him out of his daze. He grabbed the phone and glanced at it to see who was calling. It was Jasmine.

"Yo," he answered.

"Hey baby. Where you at?"

"Uh…I can't talk right now."

"Why not?"

"Look baby. I'm sorry to tell you this but I did something real stupid and the police are chasing me right now," he said as he slowed down to make a right turn onto Reames Road.

"What'chu mean?"

"Me and Black just robbed a fast-food restaurant on Sunset Road and Black's dead baby."

"What!!!

"Yes."

"Is that the reason I hear all those sirens in the background?"

"Yes."

"And what happened to Black?"

"I killed him baby." Jasmine could hardly believe what she was hearing. " I was trying to make you happy baby. I was trying to hit a quick lick to make some fast money so I could get a new place for you and our baby."

"Damn baby you didn't have to rob a damn restaurant!" Now what are we going to do?!" Jasmine yelled.

"I didn't know what else to do baby. I was only trying to please you! What else was I supposed to do?"

Jasmine began to cry. "I don't know...something... anything but rob a restaurant!"

Tariq felt bad. "Look baby, I gotta lose the police. I'll see you later tonight when I get home. I love you baby," Tariq said with no intentions of coming home.

"I love you too," she said. "And please be careful."

Tariq pressed the talk button on his phone ending the conversation. Pressing the accelerator to reach 90 mph again Tariq purposely refused to turn the stirring wheel that would have taken him around the curb. Feeling as though he had nothing to live for he allowed his vehicle to drive straight ahead crashing into the huge 100 year old tree. The impact was so great it caused Tariq's vehicle to split three different ways killing him instantly.

CHAPTER 13

It had been two weeks since Eva blurted out Jasmine was pregnant by Trey. Those words continued to play in Breeze's head over and over again and it hurt pretty damn bad. She still hadn't taken any of Trey's calls and each time he came by she had her family tell him she wasn't home. She hadn't spoken to Jasmine either. What was there to say? She felt as though she had been deceived by both Jasmine and Trey and that somebody should have said something before things went as far as they did. And maybe, just maybe it would have prevented her from falling in love with Trey. Here she was looking like Boo Boo the damn fool! She felt as though she just couldn't win for losing. Just when she thought she had found true love and someone who actually had her best interest at heart, there she was getting played. After what she had been through with Craig she just didn't need this shit in her life right now.

Breeze's heart had been tormented and aching since the day she heard the news. Part of the pain came from the mere fact that her cousin was carrying her man's baby and the other was partly because her man hadn't been honest with her. It was killing Breeze not to talk to him but she just couldn't. She had determined it was over between them. It just had to be that way because if he could be dishonest about something like that he would lie about anything. She just couldn't let herself take him back. She'd been crying every time she listened to his messages. Hell the truth of the matter was if she let him get away with this he'd think he can do anything he wants to do to her.

* * *

Breeze finally got up and showered, got dressed and left the house. After all, she had been through she just needed a breath of fresh air. She drove out to South Park mall and did a little shopping, mostly window shopping. She didn't have a whole lot of money on her but she was enjoying looking at the latest fashions displayed in the window front of the many different stores.

She made her way over to the Louis Vuitton store. After browsing around looking at the purses, she spotted her love – a beautiful Louis Vuitton scarf. Wow, $395. I'll have to save a few months to buy that, she thought.

"I'll take it," said the gentleman who was now standing over her shoulder to the sales associate standing in front of her.

"Wow, that's a really nice scarf," Breeze said to the handsome gentleman. "She must be very special," she said turning around slightly to get a better look at him, and he was fine as hell.

"What makes you say that?" he asked, smiling.

"Well that's a pretty expensive gift." He smiled again and handed the sales associate his credit card. Breeze turned to make her exit out of the store.

"Excuse me...you never told me your name," he said catching up to her.

"You never asked."

"Well?"

She smiled.

"I'm waiting," he said.

"Breeze."

"Your name matches your beauty."

"Well aren't you charming."

"You think so?"

"I sure do. So what's your name?"

"Tanner, Malik Tanner."

"Well it's been a pleasure meeting you Tanner but I have to go now."

"Awww...so soon?"

"Yeah."

"Have lunch with me."

"I can't."

"Why not?"

"I have an appointment to keep," she lied.

"Can I see you again?"

"I don't think so."

"Can I call you sometimes?"

"I don't think that would be a good idea."

"Tell you what," he said, "Take this and buy yourself some lunch." He wrote his phone number on a $100 dollar bill and gave it to her. Call me sometimes – that is if you change your mind about talking to me again."

"You're very persistent aren't you?" she said placing the $100 dollar bill in her purse.

"I am," he said smiling.

"Well it was nice meeting you but I really do have to go," Breeze said, realizing she was almost to her car. He had walked with her the majority of the way to her car. As quiet as it's kept, she was enjoying every minute of it and really didn't want to stop talking to him. But of course she had to play a little hard to get. Once she got to her car she pressed the unlock button on her key chain so she could get in. Just as she was about to close the door he grabbed the door.

"Let me get that for you," he said.

"Wow, and you're a gentleman too? Nice," Breeze said.

"And you forgot something," he said smiling.

"What'd I forget?" she asked with a puzzled look on her face.

"Your scarf," he said handing her the Louis Vuitton gift bag.

"Are you serious?" I know he didn't think I was

going to turn it down. Hell that's only on TV, she thought.

"Yes. I saw you eyeing it in the store."

"So how long were you watching me?" she asked playfully.

"Long enough to know you really wanted that scarf."

"And you made me wait all this time to give it to me?" she said lightly punching him.

He smiled and closed her door.

She cranked her car and rolled the window down. "Thank you."

"My pleasure. Hope you enjoy it."

"Don't worry, I will," she said smiling.

"Have a great lunch," he said walking away. Breeze smiled at him, rolled her window up and slowly drove away.

CHAPTER 14

Three weeks had gone by and Breeze still had not spoken to Trey. She had not returned any of his calls and each time he came by to see her she had her family to tell him she wasn't there. Jasmine had eventually told him that Eva had broke the news to her about the baby. She learned that piece of information by listening to all of his messages. Nevertheless for some strange reason she was missing him. And for the first time since she found out about the baby she decided she wanted to see him. Hesitantly Breeze picked up the phone and dialed Trey's number.

Ring! Ring! Ring! Ring!

'Yo dis ya boy Trey. Leave a message." **Beeeep.**

"Trey this is Breeze...(she paused)...um...just... um...giving you a call. Oh well, you're not available so maybe I'll call you some other..." **Beep.** She took the phone from her ear and looked at the caller ID. It was Trey beeping in on the other line. "Oh looks like that's you calling me on the other line," Breeze said finishing up her message.

"Hello?"

"Heeey baby! Damn, what's up?" Trey asked, happy to finally be hearing from Breeze.

"Not much. I just thought I would give you a call to see how you were doing."

"I'm doing much better now that I'm talking to you."

"Mmmm, okay."

"So how you been?"

"Fine, I guess. Or should I say as well as to be expected," she said asking a rhetorical question.

"I'm glad you're doing at least okay." I've been missing you and it's been driving me crazy not talking to you."

"I just wasn't ready to talk to you, Trey – or see you for that matter."

"I understand baby," he said getting silent.

"Well like I said, I just wanted to see how you were doing," she said aching inside – partly because she missed him and partly because she was still hurt about the baby.

"I need to see you baby," he said lowering his voice. Damn why the hell does he move me like this? She thought for a moment that she should play the role and not let him know how bad she wanted to see him but she had held out long enough and needed to see him. She badly needed to hear what he had to say.

"I want to see you too Trey but only to talk. I just need closure," she said trying to make it sound like it was over.

"When can I see you?"

"When you talking?"

"Is tonight good?"

"That's fine."

"Can I pick you up at seven?"

"That's fine."

"Alright I'll be there. Can't wait to see you."

* * *

After a long shower Breeze put on something simple but elegant. She slipped on a long ankle length black dress that was fitting to her body, revealing her hour glass shape. Pulled out her Chanel sandals and slipped them on. She accessorized with dangling Chanel earrings and her Chanel purse. Dabbing on some Viva La Juicy, by Juicy Couture she left out of the house to join Trey who had been waiting for her outside in his car. He had gotten there early.

CHAPTER 15

Breeze starred at the waiter as he recited the restaurants special of the day.

"Can you give us a little more time please?" she asked.

"Sure," he said. May I get you something to drink while you're deciding?" Trey looked at Breeze to go first.

"I'll have a sweet tea with lots of lemon."

"And let me have Ciroc and pineapple juice."

"Alright," stated the waiter, "I'll be right back with your drinks." They both sat there looking over the menu trying to decide what they wanted. They still hadn't said anything to each other.

"Have you two decided what you'd like to eat?" the waiter asked placing their drinks on the table.

"Yea, she's going to have her favorite, chicken gratela, spaghetti with meat sauce, and a side of broccoli," Trey answered. Breeze smiled on the inside, careful not to let him see. He remembered, she thought. "And I'll have the shrimp pasta weesie with extra sauce on the side," he said completing their order. The waiter walked away leaving them to themselves.

"You remembered," she said, unable to withhold her smile any longer.

"How could I forget?" Breeze smiled sipping her tea.

"I've missed you," he said making eye contact with her.

"Really?" she said nonchalantly. "No. I missed you like hell."

"What did you expect me to do, act like everything was honkie dorie?"

"No but I expected you to come to me and talk

to me. You could have at least told me why you weren't talking to me."

"Oh really?"

"Yeah."

"Well you sure didn't come talk to me when you found out you have a baby on the damn way."

"Okay, okay, okay. I fucked up on that. I just didn't want to tell you. Not yet anyway 'cause I don't even know if the baby is mine."

"You fucked her didn't you?"

"I mean, yeah I fucked her but damn I fucked her the first night."

"And that was it?" Breeze asked already knowing he had fucked her more than once.

"I mean I hit it a couple of times but it wasn't shit! Besides if I fucked her the first night, only God knows who else was fucking her. So how the fuck was I supposed to know the kid is mine?"

"Lower your voice, people gon' hear us."

"My bad. I'm just saying, she didn't mean shit to me. And plus I didn't even know you and her was kin till I saw her that day in your living room when you introduced us."

"Why the hell didn't you tell me then?"

"Because, Breeze it wasn't shit to tell and I didn't want to risk losing you. I thought you might stop seeing me if you knew I had been wit' her."

"Ok you're right, I would've."

"See what I'm saying?"

"I mean, do you think that's right?"

"Listen baby what we have is special, and I don't want to lose you."

"Are you serious?" she asked sarcastically. "I mean at this point I really don't know how to take you. Truth be told, you were the one who initiated the *'let's always tell each other the truth pact.'*"

"I know, I know, but put yourself in my shoes. What would you have done? Would you have told me if the shoe was on the other foot?"

"Honestly, Trey, I don't know what I would've done," she said suddenly trying to understand where he was coming from.

"See what I mean baby. I was between a rock and a hard place. I didn't know what to do."

"Chicken gratela, spaghetti with meat sauce, and a side of broccoli?" the waiter asked trying to figure out where to place the food on the table.

"That's her order," Trey replied.

"Alright and shrimp weesie pasta with extra sauce on the side is for you. Would either of you like cheese?"

"No thank you," they both answered.

"Alright, enjoy your meals. I'll be right back to refill your drinks."

"Thanks," Breeze said politely.

"Trey I just need you to understand that this is hard for me. First of all I'm not sure I can trust you anymore. And secondly, I'll have to look at this baby for the rest of my life knowing that he's the child that the man I love fathered. And what's worse is we're family! How do you think that makes me feel?"

"I know it's a lot to ask baby, but we can get through this."

"Don't get me wrong Trey, I do love you but I just don't know right now. I mean this is my first time seeing you since I found out. I don't want to make any quick decisions," she said twirling her fork in her spaghetti, suddenly losing her appetite.

"What decision do you have to make? You promised you would never leave me." She didn't respond trying to search her brain to remember when she had told him that.

"You don't remember do you?" Breeze tried to act as if she did.

"Of course I remember," she lied.

"No you don't. It was that night we went to dinner at Chima Brazilian Steak House."

"I know but this is hard for me. Right now I just want to enjoy the rest of our time tonight here together. Let's just see how things play out. Just let the chips fall where they may."

"Okay baby, I won't pressure you let's just eat and enjoy the rest of the evening with each other. By the way, did I tell you, you look stunning tonight?"

CHAPTER 16

After their dinner date Breeze loosened up a little more and snuggled up to Trey letting him hold her. But she couldn't bring herself to let him make love to her right then. He had kissed her forehead and pulled her close to him. Eventually they fell asleep. Breeze was resting peacefully only to wake up to another conversation she didn't want to have.

"You know I gotta go to court soon," Trey said.

"Yeah I know. I'm not looking forward to that."

"Me neither."

"You think you may get some time?"

"Hhhhhuh, yeah, I think so. My attorney said it doesn't look good."

"Damn Trey, why is everything spinning out of control."

"I don't know baby," he said squeezing her tighter. Breeze started to cry revealing her true feelings.

"I'm sorry baby girl. Don't cry," he said kissing her tears. "I know I promised to always be here for you, but I gotta go." Breeze continued to cry.

"Listen to me," he said raising her face with both his hands, "I love you and I'm going to take care of you no matter what."

"How you gon' do that locked up?"

"I'll only be gone for a little while. I'll leave you my car and I'll make sure Skii keeps an eye on you."

"But that's not the same," Breeze said still crying. "And besides I have my own car."

"Sh-sh-sh," he said, drowning her words with his gentle kiss. She felt his manhood rising.

"We…gon'…be…fine baby," he said in between kisses.

Breeze gasped for breath to tell him she wasn't so sure but he wouldn't let her. He drowned her words with more of his kisses. Slowly she surrendered to his touch. He slipped her right nipple into his mouth, circling around it with his tongue. He made his way down to her love box and slipped his warm stiff tongue in and out. He tickled her pearl with the tip of his tongue until she came. He then turned her over on her stomach and entered her from behind. She moaned with painful pleasure as he parted her tight walls. He slid his love muscle in and out of her over and over until he exploded inside of her. Exhausted, he laid down on her, his muscle still inside. Breeze squeezed her pussy walls relieving him of all his love juice, causing him to jerk and shiver.

CHAPTER 17

"What am I gon' do?" Jasmine asked Sheree.

"Damn girl I feel bad for you. You've been through a lot. But you know, you just gotta somehow pull yourself together and be strong."

"I know, it's just fucked up. Tariq being killed and all...then this muthafucka Trey ain't even claiming the baby. I just don't know what to do right now."

"Girl, fuck Trey."

"I know right?"

"Hell yeah! He ain't shit for that! Don't worry about his ass. Just do what you gotta do and make him pay child support."

"Oh you ain't gotta worry about that! Trust and believe I will get that!"

"I know that's right. So what's up with you and Breeze? Y'all talking yet?"

"Yeah, I mean, it is what it is."

"Riiight, riiight."

"At the end of the day she knows I fucked him before she met him. But shit who knew?"

"Riiight, riiight."

"Hell if I had known they was gon' hook up later on, after I fucked him, I would'a never fucked wit' him."

"I know....damn chile."

"Yeah she was happy as hell before she found out."

"I know. Why the hell would Eva do some shit like that anyway?"

"I don't know. It wasn't the fact that she told her, it was the way she told her. And for real, for real she should've left that up to me and Trey. It wasn't her place. I think she on some ol' jealous type shit."

"Yeah you right. It really was none of her damn business. That was fucked up tho."

"Yeah I know. But maybe she and Trey can work it out."

"And you don't care?"

"Hell no!" I don't want his ass. At this point all I want him to do is take care of his baby. I just hate it all happened the way it did."

"Yeah but you and Breeze are family. Y'all will get through it."

"Yeah I'm sure we will."

Eva rolled her eyes and eased the other phone back down on the receiver so Jasmine wouldn't notice she had been on the other end ear-hustling. They so damn stupid, Eva thought.

* * *

"Girl, are you crazy?" Queenie asked Breeze.

"I mean if loving him is crazy then call me crazy. At the end of the day, when they met neither one of them knew that Trey and I would meet and fall in love."

"Well didn't nothing stop neither one of their asses when they both were standing in that damn living room when you introduced them to each other either. They played you like a damn fiddle."

"Maybe it caught both of them off guard and..."

"Off guard my ass! Don't be so damn gullible Breeze!"

"You think this is easy for me!" Breeze yelled getting emotional.

"No I don't. Look, I'm sorry," Queenie explained feeling apologetic for getting Breeze upset.

"I know this has been a bit much for you. I just love you girl and I don't want you to have to keep going through the bullshit."

"I know girl, I 'ppreciate it. I'm just going to move on and see where it goes from here."

"And what about the baby?"

"What about it?"

"That baby gon' grow up confused as hell."

"No it's not. Not when he or she will be showered with lots of love and care."

"Okay if you say so," Queenie said sounding

doubtful.

"Girl I know I sound stupid, but I love him."

"At the end of the day, it's your life and I'm your friend. I'm with you whatever you decide. Hell if you like it, I love it." They both laughed.

CHAPTER 18

Megan ordered two steak dinners with salad and baked potatoes from late night room service for her and Trey. He had swung by her sister's house and picked her up for a late night rendezvous. While waiting for Trey to get out the shower she thought about how much she loved him. The two of them had been kicking it for the past three months. She was feeling him so much and felt that now, the feeling was mutual. Trey had told her on numerous occasions that Breeze was his main girl and that he and Megan was just kicking it. He'd told her that as long as she kept her mouth shut everything would be okay and they would have no problems. But Megan was getting tired of playing the number two position. She felt it had been long enough for him to fall in love with her and tonight would be the night she would confront him. She reminisced about the sweet love he'd just made to her. Her pussy still throbbed from his thick nine inches that he continuously made disappear and reappear in and out of her. Damn I love him, she thought as she turned over onto her side pulling the sheets up to her chin. She smiled knowing that the time was drawing near for Trey to get rid of that bitch Breeze and make her his number one instead.

Trey turned the shower off and reached for the thick white towel to dry off. He made sure he'd dried all the water from his body and wrapped the towel around the bottom of his torso. With his court case far away from his mind he was feeling on top of the world right now. He had gotten his main girl back and he had just fucked his sidekick. He couldn't wait to grab a bite to eat. He'd had Megan to order room service. He was ready to get a good night's sleep.

He walked into the room and climbed into bed with Megan. He relished at her beauty. He lay on his back and tucked his right hand behind his head resting on the pillow. Megan climbed onto him and lay on his chest, resting her arm across his buff chest. He held her close with his left arm.

"I love you baby," Megan said snuggling closer. Trey smiled, rubbing her arm acknowledging that he'd heard her.

"I said I love you baby?" she said raising her head a little.

"I know ma, that's what's up," Trey replied kissing her forehead.

"Sccch!" Megan smacked her lips and rolled her eyes.

"What's wrong?" Trey asked already knowing the answer.

"You never tell me you love me back."

"C'mon ma, we been through this a thousand times."

"Why can't you just say it?"

"Why you tryn'a force me to say something I'm not ready to say?"

"Is that your way of saying you don't love me?"

"Why the fuck you wanna talk about this shit right now? We were having a perfectly good night and you wanna bring this shit up – for the millionth time," he said sliding from under her.

"Tell me something?"

"What, damn!"

"What is it?"

"What'chu mean, what is it?"

"What is it that bitch got that I ain't got?"

"Aw fuck!" Here you go with that shit again!"

"Well what the hell is it?" Trey didn't respond.

"I'm listening." Trey got up and put his pants on, still not responding.

"So what? You leaving now?"

Tap. Tap. Tap. Since he was already up and out of the bed, Trey opened the door and retrieved the food from the bellman, tipped him and closed the door. He placed the tray of food on the table and started to put his wheat-colored timberland boots.

"So you really gon' leave?"

"Yeah if you keep this bullshit up," he finally said.

"I didn't come here for this shit."

"Okaaaay," Megan said softly, changing her strategy. "I promise I'll stop talking about it. Just don't leave baby." Starting to feel sorry for her, Trey went over and sat down on the edge of the bed. He began to stroke her head and run his fingers through her hair. He knew that she loved him and had been true to him but his heart was with Breeze. He had told Megan over and over that he cared about her but he'd also told her when he first met her he had a main girl and that he loved her. He knew this was all his fault. Lust would get the better of him time and time again but he kept fucking her knowing she was falling in love with him. Although he hardly ever took her places and would only ride her in his car at night, he kept her pockets laced with plenty of cash and bought her nice gifts. He did that to keep her mouth shut and of course to keep the flow of her sweet pussy open. He knew he shouldn't have spoiled her but he couldn't help himself.

"Look," he said, "We've been over this many times. It's not like I don't care about you, but you knew what time it was when we first started kicking it. I ain't never lie to you ma."

"I know baby, I just love you."

"I know you do baby but you have to understand...I have a woman. I told you that when I met you," he said pulling her closer.

"Fuck!" Trey said with lots of emotion. "I didn't mean for this shit to happen," acknowledging his feelings for her. He pulled her closer to him. Megan began to cry. But secretly she plotted in her mind how she would make it known to Breeze that she was in Trey's life and she wasn't going anywhere. In her mind it was time for her to become the number one chick in Trey's life. He needed to prepare anyways. Afterall, he was getting ready to be a father – Megan was six weeks pregnant.

CHAPTER 19

"What the fuck!!" Trey yelled jumping up out of the bed from his peaceful sleep. The ice cold pitcher of water Breeze had doused him with covered his face and spilled over into the bed. Quickly gaining his focus and scanning his surroundings he noticed Breeze and Megan both in the hotel room where he last remembered falling asleep with Megan in his arms.

"What the fuck is wrong with you?!!" he yelled at Breeze.

"What the fuck is wrong with me?!! How dare you!!" she shot back. I trusted you she yelled charging at him with full speed. Upon contact she swung continuously, beating him with her fists. She tried desperately to bang his face up. She swung hard as she could, releasing her pain. Trey ducked and blocked her vicious blows. He knew he'd hurt her deeply. He knew he would lose her but as he continued to block her blows he made up in his mind he wouldn't lose her again, even if he was wrong. He told himself right then and there that he would only lose her to death, even if it meant to kill her and then take his own life. By then Breeze was losing her strength – physical and emotional. She let out a gut-wrenching scream that was indicative of her deep hurt. With his mind made up, he held her while she slid to the floor pounding his chest with her fists with the little strength she had left.

"I hate you, I hate you, I hate you!" barely escaped her lips as the tears poured out of her eyes. The pain was so great she could hardly speak. Her stomach was in knots. Finally she had no more strength and just sat there on the floor while Trey held her. He felt terrible about the pain he caused her but he had made his mind up and was determined he wouldn't lose her again.

Breeze took a deep breath and tried to let out a loud scream to release more of the pain she felt, but when she opened her mouth nothing would come out. She couldn't believe she let herself trust him again. How could she have been so stupid? Her pride invaded her thoughts and at that moment she rose to her feet and wiped her eyes.

"I never want to see or talk to either of you ever again!" Breeze said just above a whisper as she headed towards the door to leave.

Megan stood there loving every moment of the damage she had caused. Serves the bitch right, she thought. Now Trey and I can be together. The previous night Megan had waited patiently for Trey to fall asleep. Once he started to slightly snore she eased out of his arms.

"Where are you going?" he asked still half asleep.

"I'm just going to get some ice water. I'm a little thirsty." Megan lied. Trey turned over getting comfortable and began to snore again.

When Megan felt he was sound asleep she grabbed his cell phone off the night stand and slipped it into her pocket. She picked up the empty pitcher and hurried out of the room. Instead of going down the hall where the ice machine was she took the elevator down to the lobby. She took the cell phone out of her pocket and scrolled down to find Breeze's name. She was puzzled when she didn't find it. She carefully searched the B's. Surely she would find *"Baby"* or *"Babe"* or even *"Bae"*, but she found nothing. Megan started getting nervous knowing Trey could wake up any minute and come looking for her. Scrolling from top to bottom she found it – it was listed under *"Wifey"*.

Bitch, Megan thought as she pressed the name

on the touch screen phone. He got some nerve calling this hoe *'Wifey'*. Jealousy gripped her as she waited for Breeze to answer.

The sound of her cell phone ringing startled Breeze waking her from her sleep.

Glancing at the clock she noticed it was 5:08 am. She grabbed the phone not even saying hello.

"Babe it's 5am, are you okay?"

"Uh, this is Megan." Breeze immediately pulled the phone from her ear to look at the caller ID because she knew damn well she had read it wrong when she first picked up the phone. When the caller ID read Hubby, for the second time, she sat up in the bed.

"Megan who, and what are you doing calling me from my man's phone? Where is he?"

"He's in our hotel room sleeping," Megan said loving the fact that she was upsetting Breeze.

"What?!"

"Look I'm not calling you to start no trouble and I don't mean to upset you but I just wanted to let you know I've been seeing him for the past three months." Heartbroken, Breeze was speechless. But just when she thought it could get no worse Megan dropped the bomb...

"I know you weren't expecting this but I felt I needed to tell you because I'm six weeks pregnant."

"And what is it you'd like me to do...is it...Megan?" Breeze asked knowing her name.

"Yeah that's my name and I really don't need you to do anything. I just thought you should know because I'm getting ready to have his baby. Stunned, Breeze couldn't believe what she'd just heard. This couldn't be happening – not again. She couldn't even respond.

"Are you there," Megan asked. Breeze held the phone, in shock and unable to respond.

"Well if you want to catch him red-handed you can come to the hotel room and see for yourself. We're at the Courtyard Marriott, downtown on South Tryon Street. The room number is 715. I'll leave your name and an extra key at the front desk. When Breeze still didn't respond, Megan pressed the end button disconnecting the call. She hurried over to the front desk, left the extra key for Breeze, stopped and got some ice cold water, and quickly went back to the room. She slid back into bed with Trey who was still fast asleep and oblivious to what had just happened. Megan lay in bed praying that Breeze would come. She was ready to become the number one girl in Trey's life.

* * *

Breeze stood in front of hotel room 715 contemplating whether or not she should use the key to enter the room. Several times she started to turn around and leave but her curiosity wouldn't let her. Nervously she stuck the key card in the door and entered the room. She was blown when she saw Megan lying on Trey's chest. Breeze quickly scanned the room to find something to hit Trey with. She knew she was done with his ass this time and he wouldn't be able to lie his way out of it. Not able to find anything right away she picked up the pitcher of ice water and doused it on him.

* * *

Whack! That was the sound that bounced off of Megan's face, snapping her out of her daydream.

"Bitch you called my girl?!" Fuck wrong wit'chu?!! He yelled hitting her again and again.

Whack! Whack! Megan stumbled and fell. Enraged Trey jumped on her and began punching her. Breeze tried with all her strength to pull Trey off of her.

"Trey stop it!" Breeze screamed. "Get off of her!" With Megan screaming under him Trey kept punching her.

"Treeeeeeeeey!!" Breeze yelled. "Please stop it! For God's sake - she's pregnant!"

The words that Breeze spat out of her mouth

114

stung Trey causing him to stop punching Megan.

"What the fuck is she talking about?"

"I...I...I'm pregnant," Megan blurted out.

"Why the fuck didn't you tell me?!"

"I was going to tell you today."

CHAPTER 20

On the drive back home Breeze cried all the way. How could he do this to me. Why didn't I see the signs. How could I have been so stupid? Why? Why? Why? What did I do to deserve this? Guess it doesn't matter anymore, it is finally over. She reached for her cell phone and dialed her best friend's number. As she told Queenie what happened she cried as the pain tugged at her heart.

"Girl I'm so sorry to hear that," Queenie said. "Damn, I just hate that for you. I knew you was too good for his ass. I knew some shit wasn't right with him. Girl he ain't shit!"

"I forgave him the first time because I love him,

but this shit is fucked up. I can't believe him," Breeze cried.

"I know girl. Are you still driving?"

"Yes."

"Why don't you come on over to my place? You don't need to be alone right now."

"Girl no!" My ass is going straight home to pack all his shit he's been conveniently leaving behind every time he comes over. It's no way in hell he can lie his way out of this one."

"I feel you girl. Just know that I'm here for you if you need me."

* * *

"Get yo' ass in the car bitch!" Trey yelled to Megan. You gon' take me to get my girl back. I'ma deal with yo' ass later!"

Megan was already sorry she had handled the situation the way she did. It had all backfired. It wasn't supposed to happen like this. She'd hoped that Breeze would leave Trey and that Trey would finally make her his girl. But things had gone wrong and now she knew he would never trust her again. And to top it all off she now feared him. He had never put his hands on her before. Her stomach began to cramp really bad but she chose to keep quiet during the remainder of the ride over to

Breeze's house.

"Pull up behind Breeze's car," Trey instructed Megan. "You stay right here till I get back. This is some shit you did so you gon' deal with it! I swear if you pull off I'ma beat yo' ass again! Trey had lost it! Clearly he wasn't himself. Megan was too scared to leave so she stayed in the car and waited.

Trey went to the trunk of the car and pulled out his sawed-off shot gun. Who the fuck she think she leaving? Told her we gon' always be together no matter what!

Bam! Bam! Bam!

"Who is it?" Breeze shouted through her bedroom door.

"Open the door," Trey said calmly, careful not to alarm her.

"What do you want Trey?"

"Open the door. I just want to talk to you," Trey said calmly.

"There's nothing to talk about. I really don't want to hear anything you gotta say Trey."

"I'm not leaving until you talk to me."

"You're making this more complicated than it needs to be. I caught you in bed with the girl so it's over! Just deal with it Trey! We're done!!!"

"Open the door, Breeze. I don't want to talk out here in the hallway in front of your family." Not thinking any harm was coming to her, Breeze unlocked the door and opened it. Trey walked through the door slowly revealing the sawed-off shot gun. Pointing the gun at her, she backed up to the wall. Scared for her life, she began to tremble.

"Didn't I tell you we was gon' be together for life?" he said, not raising his voice. Breeze shook her head up and down, meaning yes. "Answer me!" he said raising his voice through clenched teeth.

"Yes baby," Breeze answered looking down the barrel of the gun.

"So why the fuck are you packing my shit?!" Afraid to answer, tears began to roll down her face. "Answer me!" Breeze jumped.

"B-Baby I caught you in bed with that girl!"

"I don't give a fuck! I told you we was gon' always be together no matter what!"

Silence filled the room.

"Tell me you love me!" Trey demanded. "NOW!"

"I...I love you baby."

"Now tell me you won't try and pull this shit again. Tell me you won't ever leave me! I don't give a fuck what I do, you gon' always by mine!" She was convinced Trey had lost it. He had never displayed this type of behavior before. With the gun now pressed deep into her stomach with the trigger pulled halfway back, she was terrified not to answer.

"I won't ever leave you baby."

"Promise me!!"

"Yes baby, I promise," Breeze said, her voice shaking from fear.

"Now take your fucking clothes off so I can eat your pussy!"

TO BE CONTINUED...

ABOUT THE AUTHOR

Myra Y. Patterson is an Author, Psalmist, Motivational Speaker, and Advocate for victims of domestic violence and abuse. After residing in Maryland for eleven years she moved back to her hometown Charlotte, North Carolina where she was born and raised. It was there that she took a leap of faith and self published her first book Hidden Deception to start her literary career. She is also the co-owner & CEO of Chayil Models & Talent Management where she manages a host of models, actors/actresses, and multi-talented individuals.

Myra is the mother of four children Je'Maal, Ja'Mia, Jeremy, and JeVante'. She currently resides with her husband and younger son JeVante.

www.ingramcontent.com/pod-product-compliance
Lightning Source LLC
Chambersburg PA
CBHW071322130626
46556CB00004B/1711